Little Jack Rabbit and Chippy Chipmunk

David Cory

Copyright © 2023 Culturea Editions
Text and cover : © public domain
Edition : Culturea (Hérault, 34)
Contact : infos@culturea.fr
Print in Germany by Books on Demand
Design and layout : Derek Murphy
Layout : Reedsy (https://reedsy.com/)
ISBN : 9791041819645
Légal deposit : July 2023

LITTLE JACK RABBIT AND CHIPPY CHIPMUNK
LOLLYPOP SYRUP

One day as Little Jack Rabbit was hopping home to the Old Bramble Patch, he came across something sweet. And what do you suppose it was? Why, a big tin pail half full of lollypop juice, standing under a little spout that was driven into a yellow lollypop tree.

"My, but it tastes good," he said, holding his mouth under the spout to let the sap drip onto his little red tongue. "I wish I had some buckwheat cakes with me."

But he didn't, so he took a little glass bottle out of his knapsack and filled it with the sweet juice.

But, oh dear me! Just then he heard a deep growl.

"Oh dear and oh dear!" cried Little Jack Rabbit, giving a hop to one side to hide behind an old stump.

And then the deep growling voice said again, quick as a wink:

"Who's stealing my lollypop sap?"

"Nobody," answered the little rabbit, peeking out from behind the old stump. And then, would you believe it, he hopped out all the way, for there stood the Big Brown Bear.

"I'll excuse you this time," said that friendly old bear with a grin. "Come into my cave and see all the lollypops I've made from the sap of the lollypop tree."

Well, there certainly were lots and lots of little lollypops piled on the shelves.

"Do you make buckwheat cakes?" asked the little rabbit.

"Every morning," answered the Big Brown Bear, "and I just drown 'em in lollypop syrup!"

The little rabbit smacked his lips.

"If you'll spend the night, I'll give you buckwheat cakes for breakfast," said the Big Brown Bear.

And Little Jack Rabbit did, and ate so many cakes the next morning that he couldn't button up his jacket until the afternoon, when he set out once more for the Old Bramble Patch.

Well, as he was hopping along, all of a sudden, just like that, he heard some one singing:

"Little Jack Rabbit goes clippity, clop;Little Bill Bunny goes lippity, lop;Little Chip Chipmunk goes jumpity, jump,Over the hollow, moss-covered stump."

"Why, hello, Chippy Chipmunk!" cried Little Jack Rabbit, sitting up on his hind legs. "What are you doing out here? Is it time for you to come out of your nice warm burrow?"

"I guess so," answered the little chipmunk. "Old Mr. Groundhog says so, and he ought to know."

"Come over," said the little rabbit, taking the bottle of syrup out of his pocket. "Do you want to taste something you'd suppose was lollypop juice? Open your mouth and shut your eyes and I'll give you the sweetest kind of surprise."

But, oh dear me. Little Jack Rabbit dropped the cork by mistake in the little chipmunk's mouth!

(Did you ever try to get a cork out of a bottle after it had slipped 'way down inside? Well, then, just think what a time we'll have with this little chipmunk.)

DR. HERON

"What was that?" asked the little chipmunk as he swallowed the cork. But, goodness me, Little Jack Rabbit was too frightened to answer. He let the glass bottle drop to the ground, smashing it all to smithereens.

"The maple syrup was fine," went on Chippy Chipmunk, "but what was that hard little lump I swallowed?"

"Oh, please don't swell up and bust!" begged the little rabbit. "Mother says if you swallow a cork it will swell and swell inside you until you can't stand it any longer."

"What's that?" asked the little chipmunk. "Did I swallow a cork?"

"Yes, you did," sobbed Little Jack Rabbit. "And it's all my fault. I let it drop into your mouth by mistake. Of course, you didn't see it. How could you, with your eyes shut?"

Chippy Chipmunk was now thoroughly frightened. "You've murdered me, that's what you've done, Little Jack Rabbit. Oh, what shall I do?"

Just then who should come along but Dr. Heron. He had very long legs and a very long bill. All doctors have very long bills, otherwise it wouldn't pay to be a doctor.

"What's the trouble?" he asked, opening his little black bag. "Anybody sick?"

"I'm going to be," cried Chippy Chipmunk. "Oh, dear Dr. Heron, don't let me die! Please don't!"

"Stuff and nonsense! Don't talk like that!" said the big bird doctor. "Put out your tongue."

"Can you see the cork?" asked Little Jack Rabbit. The little chipmunk was just going to ask the same question, but Dr. Heron had hold of his tongue, so he couldn't.

"See what?" asked the doctor. "What are you talking about?"

"Chippy Chipmunk swallowed a cork," said Little Jack Rabbit. "And he'll swell up and bust in just a few minutes. Oh, dear, oh, dear. And it's all my fault."

"Well, I do see something," said Dr. Heron, squinting down the little chipmunk's throat. "My, but it's a long way down." And Dr. Heron looked very serious, very serious indeed.

"Now sit still and don't you sneeze.Open wider, if you please;Maybe I can pull it outIf you do not cry or pout."

Then he pushed down his long thin bill and pulled out the cork.

"Oh joy!" cried Chippy Chipmunk as soon as Dr. Heron let go of his tongue.

"I usually charge ten little fishes for an operation like this, but, seeing it's you, and I didn't have to come all the way over to your house, I'll ask only five," said the kind bird doctor.

When Little Jack Rabbit heard this he winked his tail and wagged his nose at the chipmunk, and the first thing you know away they went, leaving the doctor's bill unpaid, which wasn't a very nice thing to do. No indeed.

When we are well the doctor's billIs never even thought of, tillOld Mr. Malady comes byWith trembling hand and tearful eye.

We always should be square and true,And pay our bills when they are due.Perhaps then Mr. MaladyWill never bother you and me.

THE SONG OF PROMISE

Wintertime, you'll soon be going,With your cold winds, blowing, blowing,And your gray clouds snowing, snowing.

Soon the warm South Wind will sing,And the Blue Bells sweetly ring, — Then we'll know it's really Spring!

Mr. Merry Sun was up bright and early, and from his blue sky shone down with cheerful warmth. From his little room in the Old Bramble Patch Little Jack Rabbit awoke with a sweet song ringing in his ear. What was it? It sounded so sweet and clear that the little rabbit opened his window to listen. There it came again, across the Sunny Meadow like a song of promise. Somehow, it made the little rabbit happy, and jumping out of bed, he ate his breakfast in a hurry and then hopped over to the Old Rail Fence.

"Tir-rell-loo, tir-rell-loo!" sounded the music of a bird.

It was a beautiful whistle, clear as a silver bell, and the little rabbit took a hop, skip and jump, for somehow he felt happier than he had for a long, long time.

At first he thought it might be Jimmy Jay who was whistling. But then, he never whistled so sweetly as this. So the little rabbit hopped along, over the dry sodden grass which all winter had been pressed down tight by the heavy snow drifts, past the Big Chestnut Tree, where Chippy Chipmunk used to gather nuts, until, by and by, not so very far, he saw Blue Bird. Yes Sir. He saw the little Messenger of Spring. There he sat on the top rail of the Old Rail Fence singing away as if his heart were full of sunshine. And I guess it was, for how could he have sung so sweetly if it hadn't been?

"Spring is here, Spring is here,I'm the bearer of good cheer.

Listen to my tale of joy,Little white furred Bunny Boy.

Soon Miss South Wind will be here,And the violet will appear.

Pussy Willow by the brookYou will find if you but look.

Tir-rell-loo! Tir-rell-loo.I'm the little bird of blue!"

And as the little rabbit looked over the Sunny Meadow it seemed as if under the warm rays of Mr. Merry Sun that the brown grass turned a tender green and the trees began to murmur in the wind the half forgotten song of summer.

"Hurray, Hurrah!" cried the little rabbit, and he hopped away to the Old Duck Pond to see if Granddaddy Bullfrog had come out of his hiding place way down in the muddy bottom. But, No Sireemam. Old Granddaddy Bullfrog wasn't going to catch his death of cold by coming out too soon, neither was Teddy Turtle. They knew better, for the ice was still floating in great pieces on the surface of the water and the old mill wheel hadn't yet begun to turn around.

SPRING IS HERE

When you first hear welcome news,You can hardly keep your shoesFrom running off with both your feetAnd telling every one you meet.

This is just the way little Jack Rabbit felt on seeing Blue Bird, the sweet-voiced Messenger of Spring. To know that Spring had come, after the long hard Winter, made the little rabbit almost as happy as if it were Xmas morning.

"There comes Professor Jim Crow," exclaimed the little rabbit, looking out from the Old Bramble Patch, and then over the Sunny Meadow fluttered Redwing and Song Sparrow.

"All the birds will soon be here," laughed the little bunny, hopping out to the Sunny Meadow to look about him. Pretty soon he heard the merry whistle of Mr. Meadow Lark.

"Good-by, Little Jack Rabbit!" cried Snow Bunting. "I'm going farther North. It will soon be too warm for me!"

And then Mr. Meadow Lark whistled, "I'm here! I'm here!" And his yellow breast shone in the sunlight as bright as a new Lincoln penny!

After that the little rabbit hopped over to the Bubbling Brook, and, would you believe it, the ice was gone and the sparkling water was flowing swiftly onward to the deep blue sea!

Oh, how fast the snow was melting. Only along the Old Rail Fence or in the hollows were patches of dingy whiteness.

Up at the Old Farm the feathered folk strutted about in the warm sunshine. Even the Weathercock seemed more lively as he turned this way and that in the gentle breeze.

"Spring is coming, Spring is here,Soon the meadow will be clearOf its snowy coat of whiteAnd the grass will sparkle brightWith the dandelion andAll the yellow cowslip band.

"I must tell all my friends that Spring is here," cried the little rabbit. He just couldn't wait, you see, for them to find it out. He thought he must be a little four-footed messenger boy bunny and spread the glad tidings. So away he hopped, clippity, clip, lippity, lip, past the Barnyard where Cocky Doodle was singing his cock-a-doodle-do song, and Henny Penny was cackling over her new laid egg.

Ducky Waddles, too, was happy as could be. In a few days he would be swimming in the Old Duck Pond and standing on his head to gobble up the little fish that came too near his great big yellow bill.

"Good-by, I'm off to tell the glad news," and away went the little rabbit. Pretty soon, not so very far, he saw at the edge of the Shady Forest, on his favorite tree, Professor Jim Crow in his glistening suit of black feathers.

LITTLE MESSENGER BOY BUNNY

The Gentle South Wind in the treesIs turning buds to tender leaves,And down the crystal Bubbling BrookThe Pussy Willows nod and lookTo see if o'er the meadow greenThe Dandelions can be seen.Soon all the flowers will be hereAnd Chilly Winter disappear.

Little Jack Rabbit hopped up to the big hollow tree where Peter Possum and Mrs. Possum had slept all winter with their little baby possums. "Come out, come out! Spring is here!"

"What's that?" asked Peter Possum, sleepily. "Who's calling?"

"It's me!" laughed Little Jack Rabbit. "Mr. Merry Sun is bright and warm, and the Pussy Willows are playing with the Cattails by the Bubbling Brook." And away he hopped, for he couldn't wait another minute, he was so anxious to spread the good news.

Pretty soon he reached Woody Chuck's front door, and called through the keyhole, "Spring is here! wake up, wake up!" Woody Chuck yawned and stretched his legs, and pretty soon he opened the door, but the little rabbit wasn't there. No siree. He was far away waking up Billy Badger. And after that he hopped over to stir up Chippy Chipmunk and Billy Coon. Dear me. That little rabbit was busy, let me tell you. He just couldn't let anybody find out the good news for himself. He wanted to be the spring's little messenger boy.

All the while the Little Balmy Breezes had been dancing here and there, ringing the blue bells, blowing on the little horn-shaped flowers and whispering to the grasses and ferns.

And Mr. Merry Sun! How he did smile up in his big blue sky.

Mr. North Wind, on his whistling snow horses, had gone up to the North Pole to tell Santa Claus that everybody had forgotten all about Xmas Trees, and that Bobbie Redvest was building a nest in the old apple tree behind the Big Red Barn.

And, goodness me! I almost forgot to mention that the Weathercock had a new suit of gold paint. Yes, sir! The Kind Farmer had climbed up on a ladder with a little bottle of gold paint and a brush to make the Weathercock as bright as a new gold dollar.

Down at the Old Bramble Patch Mrs. Rabbit was housecleaning. The Old Red Rooster had taken down the storm door and stored it away in the barn. He had unwound the straw wrappers from the rose bushes and cleared away the dry leaves from the cellar door. Yes, sir. He was as busy as could be, for Mrs. Rabbit kept one eye on him all the time and he never even had a chance to crow except at two o'clock in the morning.

GRANDDADDY BULLFROG

Now round and round the Mill Wheel turns,But all the Winter through'Twas tightly bound with icy chainsTill Mistress South Wind blew.Then off it started one bright mornTo grind the farmer's yellow corn.

Granddaddy Bullfrog seated himself again on the old log to catch a fly for breakfast. All through the cold weather he had slept in the soft mud at the bottom of the Old Duck Pond, but now, that Mr. Merry Sun was shining down so warm and bright from the big blue sky, the old gentleman frog had kicked out his long legs and swam up to sit once more in his accustomed place.

But, goodness me! How thin he was. Why, his white waistcoat was all wrinkled and his pantaloons bagged dreadfully. Yes, sir. They were much too big for his long thin legs, and Granddaddy Bullfrog at once set to work to catch a million flies so as to grow nice and fat and jolly by the good old Summer time.

Teddy Turtle, too, had come up from the soft mud. He knew it was time to be about, for Gentle Spring has a way of telling all the little people of the Shady Forest and the Sunny Meadow just when it's time to wake up and get out in the warm sunshine.

And while Granddaddy Bullfrog quietly caught a dozen flies and Teddy Turtle crawled up on the bank, the little rabbit shouted:

"Helloa, helloa! There isn't much snowAnywhere to be seen, and the meadow is green.Say, Granddaddy Frog, out there on your log,Are you glad it is Spring, ting-a-ling, ting-a-ling!"

"There, you've gone and made me lose a fly," said the old gentleman frog. "But, never mind! I'm glad to see you, little rabbit," and Granddaddy Bullfrog went "Ker-dunk, ker-chunk," and wiped his spectacles with a pink silk handkerchief.

Just then from a little pool close to the Old Duck Pond came the sound of voices. "What's that?" thought the little rabbit, and he hopped over the marshy ground to look into the little pool. And what do you think he saw? Why, a lot of dark spots on the water, each one singing a tune. And, Oh dear me! The little bunny was so surprised that he leaned way over the water, when, all of a sudden, the little dark spots disappeared and all he could see were funny little forms swimming away under the water.

"Ha, ha!" laughed Granddaddy Bullfrog. "They are little singing toads. Mr. Tree Toad's grandchildren!"

The little rabbit was so surprised that he said nothing. Neither did Granddaddy Bullfrog until the next story.

RAT-A-TAT-TAT

"Well, well, well," thought the little rabbit, as he hopped away from the Old Duck Pond, "Granddaddy Bullfrog is a wise old frog." And I guess the little rabbit was right, for everybody doesn't know that those little funny singing toads I told you about in the last story are called Hylas, although everybody knows that some candies are! But it isn't spelt the same way. Oh dear me, no! But I don't believe Granddaddy Bullfrog knew that!

And while the little rabbit was hopping along towards the Shady Forest, he heard a noise like the beating of a drum. So he stopped to listen. There it came again, rat-a-tat-tat! rat-a-tat-tat! Yes, sir. Those sounds certainly came from the old orchard. So the little rabbit turned and hopped along the Old Rail Fence until he came to an old apple tree just behind the Big Red Barn where the Weathercock lived.

Rat-a-tat-tat! rat-a-tat-tat! "Who can it be?" thought the little rabbit, and he looked all around, and then, all of a sudden, he saw Red Head, the Woodpecker, building a new home for himself in the old apple tree.

Chip, chop, chip, chop, back and forth went the woodpecker's sharp bill, cutting out the chips from the old apple bough.

My! but it was hard work. The Miller's Boy always grumbled when his father told him to chop the wood, but Red Head kept right along, happy as could be. You see, the little people of the wood don't grumble if they have to work, and let me tell you in the Spring they have lots to do. Every one is busy making his home. Some are digging holes in the ground and some are making nests in the trees. But everybody is happy as the day is long. And the birds sing as they work, for a song helps the work along. Helps you do your very best, whether it's a hole or nest. Sing away, and never fret, worry won't keep out the wet. Sing and work until the sun tells you that the day is done.

Oh, dear. There goes my typewriter making up poetry!

Well, let me see where I was before my typewriter became a poet. Oh, yes. Red Head, the Woodpecker, was chopping out a little home for himself in the old apple tree, and Little Jack Rabbit had just discovered who it was who was making that queer chip-chop noise.

"Haven't got any time to talk," said the busy little woodpecker. "I must get this house ready for Mrs. Red Head. She says she won't wait another day," and he started to chop again, so the little rabbit hopped over to the Sunny Meadow where Mrs. Cow was eating the fresh young grass. Every now and then she would ring the bell on her collar, and then her little calf would run up and ask her what she wanted. And Mrs. Cow would rub her nose over the little calf's ear and whisper: "I only wanted to keep you from going away too far."

BUSY PEOPLE

The little Balmy Breezes shookThe Pussy Willows by the brookUntil they all began to mew,Just like real pussy kittens do.

And this made Mrs. Cow laugh, who, in the story before this, you remember, had tinkled the little bell she carried on a leather collar around her neck, to caution her little calf not to run too far away.

Well, just then Little Jack Rabbit came along to tell Mrs. Cow what Red Head, the Woodpecker, was doing up in the old orchard. "Yes, he's making a nice little home for Mrs. Red Head," said the little rabbit "Everybody is working but me. I'm just hopping around doing nothing," and he gave a great big sigh and scratched his left ear with his right hind foot.

"You're the first person I ever met who longed for work," laughed Mrs. Cow. "Up at the farm the men are grumbling because they must get up with Mr. Merry Sun and work all day!"

Just then Jimmy Jay flew by in his beautiful blue coat and white waistcoat. Now Jimmy Jay is a dreadful tease. He's the biggest tease in all the Shady Forest. And when he saw the little bunny, he stopped to ask a question.

"Why don't you build a house for yourself on the Sunny Meadow?"

"I don't need one," answered the little rabbit. "Old Bramble Patch, U. S. A., is where I live."

"But everybody is building a home," went on Jimmy Jay. "Why don't you get to work?" and the mischievous little bird picked off a hard round bud and threw it at the little rabbit. Then off he flew, singing at the top of his voice:

"Some folks are so lazyThey never do a thing,But bother everybodyWho's busy in the Spring."

"I wonder if he means me," thought the little rabbit. "Oh, dear me! I wonder if he means me!" and this time the little rabbit spoke out loud, for he felt so badly he just couldn't keep it to himself.

"If he does he isn't telling the truth," said Bobbie Redvest.

"He's a mischief maker," cried another voice, and there stood Timmy Meadow Mouse. "Don't let him worry you, little rabbit." After that the little bunny felt ever so much better, for what is nicer than to have your friends stick up for you in this world, I should like to know, and he hopped off home to help his mother, who was busy beating the carpets and putting up the curtains in camphor for the Summer. And after he had polished the front doorknob and fed the canary, she gave him five carrot cents and told him he might go down to the Three-in-One Cent Store to buy a raspberry lollypop.

MOTHER NATURE

"Oh, I shall be so glad when the leaves are on the trees and bushes and the Sunny Meadow is covered with grass," said Little Jack Rabbit, one lovely morning. You see, in the dear old Summer time there are thousands of hiding places, but in the Winter and early Spring everything is bare. I'm sure I don't know how this little bunny, all winter, would have escaped the eager eyes of Hungry Hawk, Mr. Wicked Weasel and Danny Fox, if his fur overcoat hadn't been white—for, of course, you haven't forgotten that his coat turns white in the Winter time, and that this is one way that Loving Mother Nature looks after the welfare of her little rabbit children. For when the snow is on the ground Little Jack Rabbit in his white fur overcoat looks like a snow ball, and at the first sign of danger he sits perfectly still, making it mighty hard for even Hungry Hawk's bright eyes to see him.

"Now, don't be wishing for something that's coming as surely as you're a foot high," said Mrs. Rabbit. "And if you're wishing for something you're not sure is going to happen, stop wishing and go out and get it," and then she patted the little rabbit on the cheek and went back to her ironing board.

As soon as he had brought in the wood and polished the front doorknob, he set off for the Shady Forest.

And by and by, after maybe a mile, he saw Jimmy Crow on a tree top. And what do you suppose that little crow was doing? Why, he was building a nest for himself. Yes, sir, that's what he was about. And why shouldn't he? For he wasn't such a very young crow now, when you come to think of it. He was a year old, and when a crow gets to be a year old he knows how to build a nest, let me tell you.

"How long will it take you, I'd like to know,To build your nest, Mr. Jimmy Crow?High up there in the tall pine tree,Where the sun is warm and the wind is free,"

asked the little rabbit.

"Don't bother me just now," answered Jimmy Crow. "Can't you see I'm in an awful hurry?" and he laid some more sticks crosswise, and then he flew away after more things to finish his nest with. So the little bunny hopped away, and pretty soon he came to the cave where the Big Brown Bear lived. And as it was a bright warm morning Mr. Bear was sitting outside on his doorstep, sunning himself, for it had been a dreadfully cold winter and Mr. Bear at one time had no coal at all, and his cave got so cold that the water pipes froze and he couldn't take a bath for a week. "How do you do this beautiful Spring morning," asked the little rabbit.

"I'll tell you in the next story," answered the Big Brown Bear. Now I wonder how he knew there's no more room in this one!

THE WHISTLING STOVE

Well, as I explained to you in the last story, the Big Brown Bear would have answered the little bunny, only there was no more room in the story for him to say even "Howdy!" So we had to wait until we turned over the page.

"Yes, it's a beautiful Spring morning. But, do you know my fur overcoat needs pressing and I'm afraid my cap's not at all in style."

"Never mind," replied the little rabbit. "Down at the Three-in-One Cent Store they have some lovely caps. Why don't you go buy yourself a new spring style?"

"I will," said the bear. "Come along with me."

So off they started, and by and by, not so very far, they came to the store, and right there in the window were lots and lots of nice looking caps. Pretty soon Mr. Bear picked out one, the one he liked best, and after he had paid for it, he and the little rabbit went outside. When, all of a sudden, who should come by but a man with a little peanut wagon. In one end was a stove that whistled the funniest kind of a song, and if I'm not mistaken the words went something like this:

Roasted peanuts, fresh and fine,Here's a lovely way to dine,Crisp and brown, and fresh and sweet,Where are nicer things to eat?Ting a ling, a ling, a loo,Won't you come and buy a few?

"Don't they smell nice?" said the Big Brown Bear and he put his right paw way down in his left coat pocket, but, oh dear me! The only thing he found was a cigar coupon. And wasn't he disappointed? Well, I just guess he was. So the little rabbit opened his knapsack and took out a handful of carrot pennies and bought two bags of peanuts. Pretty soon after the Big Brown Bear had eaten his, he said:

"Well, I must be going back to my cave," and away he went, so the little rabbit looked around to see what he would do next. But there wasn't anything to do for all he could see, so away he hopped and by and by he came to a big billboard on which was pasted a colored poster of a May Day party of little bunnies, and underneath the words:

"Enquire at Rabbitville Gazette."

Without waiting to read the other side of the billboard, he hopped down Turnip Street till he came to the Newspaper Office, when he hopped upstairs to see the advertising man — a little Field Mouse. But, oh dear me, the tickets were a dollar apiece, so Little Jack Rabbit said: "I'll give a May Day Party of my own!"

MESSENGER BOYS

The little Balmy Breezes were very busy. Indeed they were. They were busier than messenger boys, for Little Jack Rabbit had asked them to tell all his friends in the Shady Forest and the Sunny Meadow to come to his May party.

So the little Balmy Breezes had plenty to do, for the little rabbit had lots and lots of friends, let me tell you.

Well, no sooner had the little Balmy Breezes started off than they came to Granddaddy Bullfrog on his log in the Old Duck Pond.

"You are invited to Little Jack Rabbit's May party."

"All right, ker dunk, I'll come, ker plunk!" croaked the old gentleman frog, and he swallowed a big green fly that came too near, and then he closed his left eye and waited for another, for that hungry old bullfrog could eat more than twenty flies for breakfast.

And then, pretty soon the little Balmy Breezes came to the Tall Pine Tree where Professor Jim Crow had his nest.

"Oh, I'll come," he said, "never fear. And I'll bring my little black book with me, too, and read some verses to the guests," and then that old black crow put on his spectacles and opened his book, but the little breezes didn't wait, for they had no time just then to hear anything.

"There goes Squirrel Nutcracker! Come to Little Jack Rabbit's May Day Party," they cried before the old squirrel could run up to the top of the chestnut tree.

"Oh, I'll be there, don't worry," he said. "And I'll bring the Squirrel Brothers and Mrs. Nutcracker with me."

"Thank you," said the little Balmy Breezes, and off they went until they came to Chippy Chipmunk's house. He was in, and he promised to come. Then off went the little breezes again and by and by they came to the Forest Pond where Busy Beaver and Mr. Muskrat lived.

"Won't you come to Little Jack Rabbit's May Day Party?" asked the little Balmy Breezes, and of course the beaver and the muskrat answered yes.

Well, the next place the little breezes came to was the Old Farm Yard.

"Little Jack Rabbit wants you all to come to his May Party," they whispered, for Black Cat was standing in the kitchen doorway, and they didn't want him to come, you see, for fear he might spoil the fun.

"I'll come," cried Henny Penny,"And I'll bring my sister Jenny.""I'll come," said Timmy Turkey,And he looked quite fierce and perky.And Mrs. Cow said she'd come too,And so did Cocky Doodle-do.And Ducky Waddles also said,"I'll come if I'm not sick in bed."

A RUDE INTERRUPTION

Now you remember in the last story how the Little Balmy Breezes were asking everybody in the Shady Forest and on the Sunny Meadows to come to Little Jack Rabbit's May Day Party. Well, there were one or two, and maybe three, who weren't invited. And if you haven't guessed by this time, I'll tell you. Old Danny Fox was one, and Mr. Wicked Weasel was two, and, let me see, who was number three? Why, yes, of course, Old Hungry Hawk. Nobody wanted these three robbers, so they weren't invited, but that isn't saying they didn't come. But you must wait and let me tell you the story, for I nearly said something I should have kept for the last.

Well, it was almost the middle of the day by the time the Little Balmy Breezes had told everybody about the May Day Party. You see, they had to go here and there and everywhere. And the Old Brown Horse lived a long way off, and so did the Yellow Dog Tramp and the Billy Goat, who ran the ferryboat over the river.

Heigh ho, come to my party,Let us be merry, my little Jack Hearty.Blow on the whistle and make the bells ring,For it's Spring, lovely Spring.Ting-a-ling, ting-a-ling.

Well, pretty soon Mrs. Cow came across the Sunny Meadow with her little bell tinkling at her neck, and after her came Cocky Doodle and Henny Penny side by side. Then Ducky Waddles on his big, flat, yellow feet, and Turkey Tim with his big, wide-spreading tail, and right behind them came Goosey Lucy. I almost forgot her, for she was so long in curling her hair that the others started off without her.

And then from the Shady Forest came the Squirrel Brothers and Chippy Chipmunk and Professor Jim Crow, with his little black book, and the Jay Bird in his flying machine, and, oh, dear me. So many more I haven't room to tell.

"Wait for me! Wait for me!" cried a voice, and over the Old Rail Fence jumped the Brown Horse, and after him came the Yellow Dog Tramp and the Billy Goat Ferryman.

And when they were all there, the Photographer Crane from Rabbitville got ready to take a picture. He set up his camera and put his head under the black cloth, and after he had turned a little brass knob, he said in a solemn voice:

"Don't you move and don't you smile,Hold your breath a little while.Keep your eyes just where they are,Twinkle, twinkle, little star."

But, good gracious me! Just then something dreadful happened. And it just spoiled that lovely picture, for through the fence jumped Danny Fox and Mr. Wicked Weasel, and there was nobody left on the Sunny Meadow except the Crane Photographer. And maybe he won't be there on the next page.

PHOTOGRAPHER CRANE

Now, wasn't it too bad that Danny Fox and Mr. Wicked Weasel broke up the May Party! You remember they were all having their pictures taken by the Crane Photographer, who had just pushed his head under the big black cloth and was telling them all to look pleasant and not to giggle, when that dreadful fox and that cruel weasel jumped through the Old Rail Fence.

Well, of course, the Crane Photographer at first didn't know why everybody was running away, but when he pulled his head out from under the big black cloth, he knew. Oh, my, yes! When he saw Danny Fox and Mr. Wicked Weasel he didn't have to ask a single question.

"Now you can take our pictures," they said, "and if you don't we'll eat you up!"

So the poor Crane Photographer stuck his head under the cloth, but, oh, dear me! He was so frightened that his great long legs knocked together and spoiled the picture.

"Look here, Mr. Crane," growled Danny Fox, "you take a good picture or you'll never take another," and that wicked old fox grinned and showed all his long white teeth.

"Oh, please don't bite me, Danny Fox.I'll make a picture with my box,And have it framed in plush and gold,So let me live till I am old."

"All right," answered the two bad robbers, Danny Fox and Mr. Wicked Weasel, and as soon as the poor crane had taken their pictures, he folded up his camera and started back for Rabbitville.

"When will those pictures be finished?" asked Mr. Wicked Weasel, and he crept up behind that poor frightened crane and tickled his bare knee.

"Just as soon as I can get them done," he answered, and he tripped over a stone and almost dropped his camera box.

Well, after that Danny Fox went back to his den on the hillside and Mr. Wicked Weasel went home, but, of course, the May party was all over. Nobody wanted to come back that day.

"Oh, dear me," said Little Jack Rabbit, "I wish the Miller's Boy would shoot Danny Fox and Mr. Wicked Weasel."

"Don't say such things," said Mrs. Rabbit. "You must keep your ears and eyes open, and be ever on the lookout for these two bad robbers. But you mustn't wish that somebody will kill them," and the good lady rabbit bustled about and pretty soon she took out of the oven some nice hot cookies and gave two or three, and maybe four to the little rabbit, and after that the little canary bird in her cage began to sing:

"I'm safe from every harm,In my golden house.Black Cat cannot catch meLike a little mouse."

DR. QUACK

Yes, Bobbie Redvest sang to meJust now a little song,Which, if you'll wait, I will relateFor it's not very long.

He told me that the apple treeIs pink and white with flowers,And that the bees are buzzing thereAll through the sunny hours.

And, do you know, I don't think there's anything so lovely as an apple tree in bloom. For when I was a little boy I loved to lie on the grass and look up into the tree where the blossoms, pink and white, made it seem just like a big nosegay of flowers.

"Tell me, little Robin," I said, "are you never worried about anything?" And the little red-breasted bird said no. "I'm as happy as the day is long," and then he flew off to the orchard to sing to Mrs. Robin.

So I closed the window and went outside to see what Granddaddy Bullfrog was doing, for I had just heard him go "honk, honk, honk!" like an auto horn.

Well, sure enough, there was the old gentleman frog, and who do you suppose was after him? You'd never guess, so I might as well tell you right away.

Why, it was Dr. Quack, the wise old duck doctor. He was on his way to see Little Jack Rabbit, who had the whooping cough, and of course his mother, the dear old lady rabbit, was dreadfully worried.

Well, pretty soon Dr. Quack stopped at the Old Bramble Patch, and with his little black bag, went inside to see the little sick bunny boy.

And of course Mrs. Rabbit was dreadfully upset. She couldn't think of anything but her little bunny boy, and the tea kettle had burned a great hole in its bottom and she couldn't make a cup of tea for the doctor, although he was very fond of carrot coffee.

"Let me see your tongue," said Dr. Quack. So the little rabbit put out his tongue, and then the wise duck doctor took out some little pills and three little white powders and told Mrs. Rabbit to give them to her little bunny every other minute and even oftener if he kept on coughing.

And then Dr. Quack said good-by and went over to the old barnyard to see Henny Penny, who had the chickenpox.

Well, after swallowing two powders and three and a half pills the little rabbit felt perfectly well. Wasn't that wonderful medicine the old duck doctor gave him? Well, I just guess it was, and if you ever get the whooping cough you call him up on the telephone, "Oh, oh, oh. Come quick, Duckville!" and he'll cure you in less than five hundred short minutes.

BY THE BUBBLING BROOK

Up at the Old Farm Yard there was a great bustle. Yes sireebus. And the reason was that Henny Penny had a brood of fluffy little chickens. Cocky Doodle hardly knew what to make of them. You see, he was so used to big chickens that when he came to look at these fluffy balls of yellow down he didn't know what to do. So he just stood on his tiptoes and crowed, "Cock-a-doodle-do!" and the big farmer thought he was singing because he was a proud father. But that wasn't the reason at all.

"Come, my dears," said Henny Penny to her little chicks, "let us take a walk in the Sunny Meadow." So all the little chickens followed after her and by and by they came to the Bubbling Brook where swarms of flies darted over the water. And every time a fly came anywhere near Henny Penny she snapped him up and divided him among the brood.

Well, pretty soon along came Little Jack Rabbit with his knapsack on his shoulder and his striped candy cane in his right paw. For it was a lovely day in May and the little rabbit was as happy as two sticks and maybe three or four.

Just then Teddy Turtle crawled by, with his little shell house on his back, and although it was the first of May, Teddy Turtle wasn't going to move out of his house. No sireebus. But his house was moving with him. But that's another matter, you see.

"Wherever I go my house goes, too,And I never pay any rent.My little shell house goes ever with me,No matter how far I am sent."

"Ha, ha," laughed the little rabbit, "you're a lucky fellow." And then Henny Penny clucked to her little brood and said, "Look at Teddy Turtle with his house on his back. Isn't he lucky?"

After a while Mrs. Cow with her tinkling bell came by, singing a song:

"Oh, the grass is nice and green,And in the Bubbling BrookI see a very nice kind faceMost every time I look."

And then she rang her little bell over and over again, just to make a noise, I guess, and after that the little rabbit hopped down to the Old Duck Pond to talk to Granddaddy Bullfrog.

Now Granddaddy Bullfrog was a wise old gentleman frog. He knew lots and lots of things, but like a good many wise people he never said much. He was usually too busy catching flies.

But when he saw the little rabbit he took off his yellow rimmed spectacles and said:

"How are you this lovely spring day, little rabbit?" and then he swallowed a fly that came too near, and after that he blinked his eyes and then he closed them to fool some other foolish fly who might happen along.

But of course he didn't close them tight shut, for then he wouldn't be able to see anything, you know. And after that the little rabbit said, "I'm very well, thank you, Granddaddy Bullfrog.

"I manage to keep very wellAnd hop up with the rising bell.My appetite is very keenBecause I never eat between

"My meals; and that's the reason whyI can digest green apple pie,And ice cream cones and lollypopsAnd Tootsie Wootsie chocolate drops.

"Now, if you're hungry, hurry on — But don't make a mistake — You'll find a bag of peanuts onPage number 88!"

HAPPY DAYS

Well, you remember in the last story little Jack Rabbit was making a call on Granddaddy Bullfrog at the Old Duck Pond. And I guess the little rabbit might have stayed until half-past thirteen o'clock if, all of a sudden, Old Sic'em, the farmer's dog, hadn't come along. Now, of course, Old Sic'em was too old to run very fast, but just the same the little bunny wasn't going to give him a chance to catch him, so off he went, clippity clip, hippity hip, and by and by he came to the Shady Forest, where all the little four-footed folk and the feathered people were busy making homes for the Summer.

Old Squirrel Nutcracker sat outside his doorstep while Mrs. Nutcracker hung out the rugs and beat the sofa cushions. And Chippy Chipmunk chattered on the top of the Old Rail Fence at Bobbie Redvest, who had flown over from the Orchard to stretch his wings.

"Tra la la, tra la la!Where's the little Twinkle Star?Mr. Merry Sun's on highIn the meadows of the sky,And the dandelions winkAll along the river's brink."

You see, Bobbie Redvest loved to sing all sorts of songs, and that's why all the little people of the Shady Forest loved him so. For we all love to hear a song if it's not too slow and long.

"Cock-a-doodle-doodle-do,Clouds are white and skies are blue,And the little bugs and fliesAre a dinner that we prize,"

sang Cocky Doodle, for he wasn't going to have Bobbie Redvest be the only one who could sing a song, let me tell you.

And just then Old Professor Jim Crow flew by with his little Black Book under his wing, and as soon as he saw the little bunny, he perched himself on a stump and turned to page forty-three:

"When you're young it's time to learn,When you're older you must earn."

And the Old Gentleman Crow took off his spectacles and said: "Do you hear that?" and then he cawed three times and a half and put his spectacles back into the case and closed his little Black Book.

"Yes, sir," answered the little rabbit. "Every day I learn something. Only this morning I found out that my last Summer's straw hat won't do for this Summer," and then he hopped away as fast as he could for he knew that Professor Crow would think it was very ex-trav-a-gant not to wear last year's hat, no matter how shabby it was.

"Clean your last year's panama,Wear your last year's suit,Don't replace a single thingExcept a worn-out boot."

Now who do you suppose sang that little verse? You'll never guess, so I'll tell you right away. Grandmother Magpie!

"I'm sorry I can't wait," said the little rabbit, and off he hopped for the Old Bramble Patch to ask his mother if she were going to clean her last year's panama bonnet.

THE HOUSE IN THE WOOD

"I wonder where I'm going to stay to-night," said Little Jack Rabbit to himself one late afternoon, after traveling all day with his knapsack on his back and his striped candy cane in his right paw, and just then he came in sight of a little wooden house. So he stopped and tapped on the door, rat-a-tat-tat, very softly, you know. And when the door opened a little monkey dressed in a red cap and a green coat said, "What do you want?"

"I beg your pardon," answered the little rabbit, "but, you see, it's getting late and I'm looking for a place to sleep."

"Well, come right in," said the little monkey, and after Little Jack Rabbit had hung his knapsack and striped candy cane on the hatrack in the hall he followed the monkey into the sitting room.

Well, after a little while he told the monkey all about the Old Bramble Patch and Danny Fox and Mr. Wicked Weasel, and lots of other things, too, which I haven't room in this story to mention. And when he had finished the monkey said he had once belonged to a man who owned a hand organ and went about the country playing music for pennies, and sometimes for nothing.

"But that was long ago," said the little monkey, "for one day my master beat me so cruelly that I ran away to the wood, and by and by I built this little house, where I have lived ever since." Just then a knock came at the door and who do you suppose was outside? Why, the Yellow Dog Tramp, the little rabbit's friend, you remember.

"Come in," said the monkey, for the Yellow Dog Tramp had stopped at his house lots of times, you know.

"Goodness me," said the Yellow Dog Tramp, after he had hung up his old tattered hat in the hall. "I was nearly arrested to-day by a policeman cat. They don't allow tramping any more. Everybody must work, so I stopped in to see if you didn't want a handy man about the place." And this made the little monkey laugh like everything, and pretty soon the Yellow Dog Tramp got dreadfully sulky. He dropped his ears and hung his tail, and then he began to whine,

"Now just because I've been a trampThrough sunshine and through fog,You needn't laugh, nor joke and chaff'Cause now I want a job;For Uncle Sam says to each man,'Now that the war is over,Each do your part with willing heart,And we shall be in clover!'"

"That's the way," shouted Little Jack Rabbit, and on the next page you shall hear what happened after that.

THE YELLOW DOG TRAMP

Well, after the monkey learned that the Yellow Dog Tramp wanted to go to work to help Uncle Sam and Aunt Columbia, as I mentioned in the story before this, he said:

"You can whitewash the back fence if you want to. It may take you a week or it may take you a month, for I don't know how fast you can work."

"Well, I'll start right in," said the Yellow Dog Tramp bravely, and he stood up on his hind legs and wagged his tail.

"You'd better wait until to-morrow morning," said the monkey. "It's too late now, and you couldn't see in the dark."

"I should think one could whitewash in the dark," said the tramp dog. "But just as you say," and he went over to the kitchen stove and lay down on the little rag rug and went sound asleep, for he was very tired, because he had tramped all day long.

"Let him sleep," said the little monkey in a whisper. "He looks tired out." And after that the monkey got the supper ready and when everything was nice and hot and on the table the Yellow Dog Tramp opened his eyes and yawned and pretty soon he was wide awake enough to sit down to eat.

Well, by and by it was time to go to bed, so they all went to sleep, and just about midnight a big owl looked in through the window and saw by the light of the silvery moon Little Jack Rabbit and the monkey sound asleep on the bed.

"Ha, ha," said the big owl to himself, "I must get that little bunny." So he perched himself on the roof and pondered how to get inside the little house.

Well, by and by, after he had flown around and peeked through all the windows, he looked down the chimney. And then he carefully stepped over the edge and, spreading out his wings, jumped right down to the bottom.

But, goodness me. When he rolled from the hearth into the sitting room he looked just like a crow, he was so covered with soot, and it would have taken the Gold Dust Twins twenty-three days and one night to clean him.

"What's that noise?" barked the Yellow Dog Tramp, and he ran in from the kitchen and looked all around. At first he didn't see the owl, for he was so black with soot, you know. But what that Yellow Dog Tramp said when he did see that bad Owl I'll tell you in the next story, unless,

The Gold Dust Twins with a scrubbing brushShould scour that old Sooty Owl,All through the night until he was brightAnd clean as a snow-white fowl.

PRICKLY THORNS

"What kind of a blackbird are you?" asked the Yellow Dog Tramp when he saw the bad owl who had flown down the chimney of the little monkey's house, as I mentioned in the last story.

"I'm not any kind of a blackbird—I'm an owl," answered this dreadful old bird, and he shook himself till the soot flew all over the room, and some of it got in the Yellow Dog Tramp's eyes and made him blink. And of course all this noise woke up the little monkey and Little Jack Rabbit, who were sleeping upstairs, you remember.

"I wonder what's going on," whispered the little monkey, and he leaned over the banisters. And just then the Yellow Dog Tramp said, "Well, you get out of here!" and he took hold of that sooty old tooty owl and threw him, tail first, out of the door. And then he threw a milk bottle after him.

When the little rabbit and the little monkey heard what had happened, they were very grateful to the Yellow Dog Tramp, and told him he could sleep all next day in the sun instead of whitewashing the back fence.

Well, after a while, after breakfast, you know, the little bunny set off again on his travels, and by and by, not so very far, he came to a place where so many wild roses grew that it looked like a lovely garden.

"Now here is a nice place to rest," he thought, and he sat down and opened his knapsack and took out a lollypop and was just going to bite off the lemon top, when somebody took it right out of his paw.

"Ha, ha, ho, ho," laughed a trumpety kind of a voice, and when the little bunny looked around he saw his old friend the Circus Elephant with a bouquet of roses in his long trunk. "Here's your lollypop," said the elephant, and he dropped the bunch of roses, for he only meant to tease the little rabbit for a minute, you know.

And then he came over and sat down. But, oh dear me. He jumped up in an awful hurry, for he had sat on the bunch of roses.

"Oh, dear and oh dear again," he cried, "why do lovely roses have thorns?" and he wiped a tear from his eye with the end of his ear, and then he sang this song:

"Oh, why should roses red have thornsAnd pears have prickly prickles,And Mr. Dill his glass jars fillWith sour little pickles?"

And after that my typewriter says you must wait a little while to hear what happened next, because

The Circus Elephant took so longTo finish this beautiful pickle song,The clock struck twelve before he was through,The Old Red Rooster woke up and blewTwice six times on his big tin horn,And nearly deafened the ears of corn.

BAGS OF PEANUTS

Well, as soon as the Circus Elephant had finished the song in the last story he took a silk handkerchief out of his trunk and wiped his eyes, and then he said: "Do you suppose, if I kneel down you can hop up on my back?"

"I'll try," answered the little rabbit. So the big circus animal squatted down on the ground, till with a hop, skip and jump the clever little bunny landed right in the middle of his back.

"Now hold on tight," said Elly, for that was the Circus Elephant's name, and off he went and by and by he came to a place where there were many peanut vines.

"Well, this is lucky," said the elephant. "We can take them to Chippy Chipmunk. I'll dig the vines and you can pick out the peanuts and fill your knapsack." So the elephant started in, and in less than thirteen minutes he had plowed up the whole field of peanuts. And in less than thirteen seconds the little rabbit had his knapsack full, but then he didn't know what to do with all the rest of the peanuts.

And while he was looking around to find a bag or a box, who should come by but the old dog with his stage coach and team of billy-goats.

"Plenty of peanuts," said the old dog driver, jumping down from his high seat and walking over to the Old Rail Fence. Then he put his old pipe back in his mouth and puffed out a cloud of smoke.

"Load up your stage coach," said the Circus Elephant, "and we'll take them to Chippy Chipmunk!"

"All right," answered the old dog, and he went back and brought over fourteen empty mail bags, and when they were brim full he put them back in the stagecoach, and then the elephant and Billy Bunny got on top, and away went the Billy Goat team.

Over the hills and through the dellsTill the peanuts rattled inside of their shells.

And by and by, pretty soon, not very long, they came to the old Chestnut Tree, where the little chipmunk lived. "Now you keep these peanuts till the circus comes," said Little Jack Rabbit. "Then all the little people in the Shady Forest can have all they want. Maybe by that time I can get lollypopade from the Big Brown Bear!"

The Big Brown Bear made LollypopadeFrom the fruit of the Lollypop Tree in the glade.Sometimes it was yellow, and often bright pink,But never the color of purple green ink.

Perhaps some fine day when out walking with meWe may happen to come to this Lollypop Tree.In that case, my dear little friends, no excuseShall keep us from tasting this Lollypop juice.

THE MUSICAL ALARM CLOCK

Chippy Chipmunk sat on the Old Rail Fence, his little eyes shining like bright glass beads, looking over toward the Old Bramble Patch.

Chippy Chipmunk felt very fine this particular morning. Mr. Merry Sun shone down on the little chipmunk's back with its beautiful smooth shining stripes of reddish brown and black, over which his little tail was thrown like a ruffle.

"Helloa, helloa!" he shouted, for I guess the Little Jack Rabbit had overslept himself that morning. "Helloa, Helloa!"

"Here I am," answered the little bunny, hopping up to the Old Rail Fence. "What do you want?"

"Oh, nothing in particular," answered Chippy Chipmunk. "Only I was wondering why you weren't around, that's all."

"I guess I'm late. You see, my Alarm Clock didn't wake up either," and the little rabbit laughed. And just then they heard it ring, "Cling, cling, cling, cling cling!" And then it began to sing:

"The dew is shining on the grass'Tis time to be awake.The Morning Glory on her vine,The Lily on the lake,Have lifted up a dewy head,—So hurry, tumble out of bed."

"Come on, Chippy Chipmunk," said the little rabbit when the Alarm Clock stopped singing, "Let's go for a walk up the Shady Forest Trail." So off they started together and after a while, not so very far, they came to the tree where Squirrel Nutcracker lived with his family. But Old Squire Nutcracker wasn't at home, and neither was Mrs. Nutcracker, and of course the two Squirrel Brothers were away. So the little rabbit and the little chipmunk went along until they came to the Forest Pond in the middle of which on a little island stood the big chestnut tree where Old Barney Owl had his home.

"He sleeps all day," laughed the little bunny, "so he's at home!"

"But how are we to get over to the island?" asked Chippy Chipmunk. But the little rabbit didn't answer. He was too busy pushing a log into the water.

"Get aboard," he said to the little chipmunk, and then with a shove he hopped on and pretty soon they reached the island, when they hopped off and up to the big chestnut tree to knock on Old Barney Owl's front door.

"Oh, Mr. Owl, pray do not scowlBecause we've called on you.It's just a surprise, so open your eyes.Please, Mr. Barney, do."

Now of course Little Jack Rabbit and Chippy Chipmunk knew that Old Barney Owl couldn't see in the daytime, otherwise they wouldn't have called on him. For Mr. Barney Owl loved to eat little rabbits and chipmunks.

MORE ADVENTURES

Now when Old Barney Owl heard Little Jack Rabbit and Chippy Chipmunk knock on his front door, he winked and blinked. But he didn't open it, for the light hurt his eyes, you know, and all day long he kept the shades pulled down.

"Who are you and what do you want?" he asked in a sleepy voice.

"It's me and Little Jack Rabbit," answered the little chipmunk.

"Come 'round this evening," replied the wise old owl.

"No, thank you," laughed Little Jack Rabbit. "We don't make calls in the evening," and he and the little chipmunk hurried away for they thought, maybe or perhaps, Old Barney Owl might open the front door and catch them.

"He, he," said Chippy Chipmunk, "he asked us to call this evening, did he? Not if my name is Chipendale Chipmunk!"

Well, after they had called on Mrs. Water Rat, who lived nearby in a lovely garden of water lilies, they hopped on board the log and after a shove, away it went over the water to the other bank, where these two little four-footed sailors hopped off and then, all of a sudden, just like that, a voice said:

"Don't you go another inchOr your noses I will pinch."

"Who said that?" inquired the frightened little rabbit.

"Who are you?" asked trembling Chippy Chipmunk.

And then Teddy Turtle crawled out from behind some bulrushes and began to laugh. And the little rabbit and the little chipmunk would have been frightened if it hadn't been Teddy Turtle, let me tell you, for some turtles are dreadful snappers, you know.

"Oh, it's you, is it?" and the little rabbit told Teddy Turtle all about the little snail at the seashore who carries his shell house around with him. "Yes, he takes his little house with him just the way you do."

"I'm going to take a swim, so good-by!" answered Teddy Turtle, crawling over to the water, and in he went with a loud splash that frightened two little minnows almost to death.

Oh, the little minnows swimWhere the water's cool and dim,'Neath the weeping willow branchesMaking shadows here and there.Where the gnats and little fliesAre making nice mud pies,And Mrs. Muskrat combs her silky hair.

"Come on, let's be going. There's always something to see. Why, here comes the Little Balmy Breezes across the Sunny Meadow," cried the little rabbit, but the little chipmunk ran off to the Shady Forest.

AT THE FARM

Across the Sunny Meadow grassThe little breezes love to pass,They tickle all the cattails tillThey almost fall into the rill.And every now and then they tellOld Mrs. Cow to ring her bell.

Now before I go on with this story I'll explain right away that the "rill" is the Bubbling Brook, and the only reason I used "rill" is because it rhymes with "till."

"Ha, ha," laughed Little Jack Rabbit, as Mrs. Cow shook her head till the bell on her collar made so much noise that her little calf came running toward her, "I heard what the little breezes said." And then Mrs. Cow gave a long "Moo!" which meant something I'm sure, for after that the little rabbit hopped away and by and by he came to the Barnyard where Cocky Doodle every morning sang his cock-a-doodle-do song to wake up Mr. Merry Sun, who goes to sleep in the West and gets up every morning in the East. I wonder how he does it, don't you? I guess you and I would feel very funny if some morning after having gone to sleep in our own bed we should wake up in another!

"Helloa," said Henny Penny, as the little rabbit hopped through the Old Rail Fence. "Where have you been all this time?"

"Oh, lots of places," he replied. "Chippy Chipmunk and I have been sight-seeing, and the Old Red Rooster has sprained his left leg and the Old Brown Horse has a new collar, and Grandmother Magpie has gone away to visit in Birdville, U. S. A."

Just then Ducky Waddles came waddling by, after a swim in the Old Duck Pond, where Granddaddy Bullfrog lived.

"I saw Teddy Turtle a minute ago," said the little duck; "he's very proud because Mrs. Turtle has just laid some eggs in a hole in the ground and covered them with dirt. He says pretty soon they'll hatch into little turtles!"

"Ha, ha," laughed the little rabbit, "don't tell that to Peter Possum; he just loves turtle eggs." So Ducky Waddles promised he wouldn't, and after that the little rabbit hopped away, although the Weathercock on the Old Red Barn had asked him to stay a little longer.

"No, I can't," replied the little bunny. "I'm afraid Old Sic'em might chase me." But even if that old dog had, the little rabbit could have slipped away, for Old Sic'em had the rheumatism and could hardly run.

Well, after a while, not so very long, the little rabbit saw Professor Jim Crow.

"Wait a minute," said the good professor, "I want to read you something." So the old gentleman crow turned to page 23 of his little Black Book, after putting on his spectacles, of course, for he couldn't see to read without them, and then he cleared his throat and said, "Caw, caw," two or four times, and looked at the little rabbit, but what he read out of his little Black Book I'll tell you in the next story.

DANNY FOX

Well, since the old crow has opened his little Black Book in the story before this, I'll tell you now what he read on page 23:

"Little brown rabbits have all the same habits."

"Ha, ha," laughed the little bunny, "you're a very wise bird, Professor Crow!" and he hopped away until he came to the wooded hill where Danny Fox had his den.

Now it was a long time since the little rabbit had seen the old robber fox and he was a bit curious to learn what was the trouble, for trouble there must have been, otherwise Danny Fox would have been around to steal a chicken now and then from the Old Barnyard.

So the little rabbit hopped along very carefully and by and by he came to a big tree quite close to the pile of rocks under which the fox family had their den, Danny Fox and Mrs. Fox, Bushy Tail and Slyboots, their two little sons.

"I don't see anyone around," said the little rabbit to himself, and he hopped over to another tree and peeped out.

And then, Oh, my! how his heart went pitter-pat, for right in front of him, not forty hops away, sat Danny Fox on a three legged stool smoking a corncob pipe.

"Oh, dear!" thought the little rabbit, "I didn't mean to get so close!" But when he saw that Danny Fox's left foot was bandaged up in a piece of white cloth with a big red cross stamped on it, he knew the old robber couldn't run very well, and maybe not at all. So he called out, "Helloa, Danny Fox! What's the matter with your foot?"

"Don't bother me," grumbled the old robber fox, not even looking around. Maybe he didn't want to see a nice fat little rabbit when he couldn't catch him for supper.

Just then Peter Possum shouted from his tree house:

"Old man robber, Danny Fox,Caught his foot in a steel trap box."

"Keep quiet, will you," snapped Danny Fox, angrily.

"Ho, ho, ha, ha," laughed the little rabbit. "So you got caught for all your slyness?" which made the old fox so angry that he jumped up and ran at him on three legs.

"Who's laughing now?" cried Danny Fox, as the little rabbit hopped away and Peter Possum climbed a tree. "You're very brave when you're out of danger," and the old robber limped back to his stool and lifted up his wounded foot. And while he was doing this, Grandmother Magpie came by, and as she was always poking into other people's business, she asked what was the matter. "If I told you," snapped Danny Fox, "everybody in the Shady Forest and the Sunny Meadow would know it in a few minutes, you old tattle tale!"

"Gracious me!" exclaimed the mischievous old blackbird, "you're in a disagreeable mood to-day," and away she flew after Little Jack Rabbit, but before she caught up to him, he hopped into the Old Bramble Patch for the night.

Wind the clock, it's time for bed;Dreams are waiting, Sleepy Head.

Through the window bright and farShines the silver Twinkle Star.

Oh, how soft the pillow lies!Cuddle down, dear Sleepy Eyes,

Underneath the counterpane,Till the robin in the lane

Sings his morning roundelay,And it's time again for play.

CHIPPY CHIPMUNK'S STORE

Chippy Chipmunk stood outside his store waiting for Little Jack Rabbit to come along. He had promised, if the little bunny would call after business hours, to help him get a little store of his own.

Mr. Chippy Chipmunk looked very nice and well-to-do in his clean striped jacket as he sat on the wooden bench just under the big sign. Pretty soon he stood up to look at it again. He had done this very same thing at least ten times that day, he was so proud of it.

"A mighty nice sign!" he said aloud, as he sat down again on the wooden bench. All of a sudden the thumperty-thump of little feet made him look up.

"Good evening," said Chippy Chipmunk.

"I was afraid I'd be late," answered Little Jack Rabbit. "You see, I had to wait until mother got home."

"Come over and sit down," said Chippy Chipmunk.

"Wait till I read the sign over again," answered the little bunny. "Wouldn't I be proud if I had a little store! I don't know what I'd sell, but that doesn't make so much difference — it's having your own name over the door that makes you feel like a millionaire."

"Come in and see the nuts," said the little chipmunk, after a while.

A long hollow log, carefully split in two, made a very nice counter. Indeed, it served also for a showcase, for in the hollow the nuts were arranged in separate piles.

"I made all the tags myself," said Chippy Chipmunk proudly, pointing to small squares of cardboard on which were printed: — CHESTNUTS — HICKORY NUTS — WALNUTS — BEECH NUTS.

"Are these your scales?" asked Little Jack Rabbit admiringly.

"Yes, I sell by the pound. Then nobody gets cheated," answered the little chipmunk, cracking a nut with his sharp teeth. "You ought to have a store at the edge of the Old Bramble Patch, with a sign painted in red and green letters:

"Do you think I know enough about vegetables?" asked the little rabbit anxiously.

"Just as much as I do about nuts," replied Chippy Chipmunk.

But, oh, dear me! If they had known what was going to happen I guess they never would have talked so long about the nut and vegetable business.

NAUGHTY FEATHERHEAD

Yes, Sir! If Little Jack Rabbit and Chippy Chipmunk had known what was going on outside the store I guess they never would have talked so long about the nut and vegetable business. For, oh, dear me! as the little rabbit shook paws good-night and looked up once more to admire the sign above the door, it wasn't there. No—nothing was there but the bare boards. With mouth and eyes wide open he stood staring at the spot where the sign had hung only a few minutes before.

"What's the—?" Chippy Chipmunk didn't finish. After he had looked up there wasn't any use in asking Little Jack Rabbit what was the matter. The answer was right before him. Poor Chippy Chipmunk!

"Who could have taken my sign?" he asked at last in a trembling voice. But, of course, the little rabbit didn't know.

"Who could have taken the sign?" Chippy Chipmunk repeated mechanically. Then he looked up again as if expecting the sign to shine forth in the old familiar way:

They hadn't heard Featherhead, the naughty son of Squirrel Nutcracker, take down the sign. Very softly, one at a time, he had loosened the screws and then carried it off and thrown it in a deep hole.

It was certainly a very mean thing to do, but then, you must remember, Featherhead was not a nice sort of a squirrel.

Just then, who should come by but Featherhead himself.

"What's the matter?" he asked, just as though he didn't know. Wasn't that deceitful of him?

Little Jack Rabbit didn't answer. Somehow he didn't quite like the little squirrel's tone of voice—it didn't ring true. And when Featherhead turned his back, showing a long streak of white paint across his shoulder, the little rabbit didn't wait a minute, but, quicker than a wink, caught the frightened squirrel and shook him till his teeth rattled.

"What did you do with Chippy Chipmunk's sign?"

"I—I threw it in a deep hole near the Tall Pine Tree," mumbled Featherhead, now thoroughly frightened.

"You come with us and get it," screamed Chippy Chipmunk, mad as a dozen hornets; and they marched the naughty squirrel over to the Tall Pine Tree.

When the sign was once more over the door Chippy Chipmunk said to his little rabbit friend:

"You got my sign back for me. To-morrow I'll help you build your store."

LITTLE JACK RABBIT'S STORE

In a few days Little Jack Rabbit's store was finished, and all the Little People of the Shady Forest and Sunny Meadow were coming to the grand opening. It stood just at the edge of the Old Bramble Patch, on the corner of the Shady Forest Trail and the Old Cow Path.

A nicely painted post had been set in the ground, on which was fastened a sign printed in large letters:

In the doorway, between barrels of cabbages and turnips, stood Little Jack Rabbit, a smile on his face and a clean white apron over his little khaki trousers. His kind mother had made two of these nice aprons so that he would always have one to wear while the other was in the wash.

You may be sure he felt very proud as he stood, bowing and smiling to his friends who had come to wish him success in his new business.

"Too young to run a store," snapped Grandmother Magpie.

"If he's as honest with his scales as he is truthful with his words," answered Granddaddy Bullfrog, looking at her through his yellow-rimmed spectacles, "all his friends will buy here."

Mrs. Rabbit was tickled to death to think that her son at such an early age had started in business all by himself. It meant to her that he would become a multi-millionaire in a few years!

Chippy Chipmunk had left his store in charge of his brother so as to be on hand, and Featherhead stood at a little distance, enviously watching the friendly greetings.

Everybody was there, even Old Parson Owl, winking and blinking, from a shady spot in the forest, nodded pleasantly and wished the little rabbit good luck.

Suddenly a sharp bark came down the Shady Forest Trail, and the next instant Old Sic'em and the Farmer's Boy jumped over the Old Rail Fence.

Into the Old Bramble Patch went Little Jack Rabbit and his mother, while the Forest Folk either ran off or flew away.

"What's this?" cried the Farmer's Boy, kicking over the cabbages and turnips that the poor little rabbit had so carefully placed in front of the store.

Down fell the sign from the nicely painted post. Crack! it went under the heel of the Farmer Boy's shoe.

"Why didn't you catch 'em, Sic'em?" he asked crossly. Then he turned away and went whistling down the path.

"I don't feel much like whistling," said Little Jack Rabbit, "my store has all gone to smithereens!"

But Mrs. Rabbit didn't say anything. I think she was even more disappointed than her little bunny boy.

BILLY BREEZE

"Billy Breeze, Billy Breeze!Come and help me, if you please.If you'll only shake the tree,There'll be lots of nuts for me."

This is what Chippy Chipmunk sang one morning when he found there were no more nuts on the ground.

Of course, he had a lot already stored away, but he didn't want to use them now. No, indeed; not until the cold weather came. Pretty soon he commenced to sing again:

"Billy Breeze, Billy Breeze!Come and help me, if you please.Shake the nuts from off the tree;Do this favor, please, for me."

Now everybody in the Shady Forest liked Chippy Chipmunk. In the first place, he was such a good little worker. Then, too, he minded his own business and was never cross. So as soon as Billy Breeze heard him call, he blew in from the Sunny Meadow and shook the tree. Down came the nuts, pitter, patter, all over the ground, and one hit the little chipmunk right on the head.

"Ouch!" he cried.

"Whew! Did it hurt?" whistled Billy Breeze.

"Well, I should say so," answered Chippy Chipmunk. "Wait till I hide before you shake again."

Then Billy Breeze gave the big tree another shake. Pitter, patter, pitter, patter! went the nuts on the dry leaves.

"I guess that's enough," said Billy Breeze. "I must go now!"

"What for?" asked the little chipmunk.

"To turn the Weathercock."

And off went Billy Breeze across the Sunny Meadow, to the Old Farm Yard. The Weathercock on the Big Red Barn saw him coming and whirled around on his gilded toe. And Henny Penny at once set to work to prune and oil her feathers. She rubbed her bill over the little oil sack hidden among the feathers on her back and said to Cocky Doodle:

PITTER, PATTER

As soon as Billy Breeze had turned the Weathercock on the Big Red Barn, he hurried away to get the rain-clouds. He didn't even wait to say howdy to Ducky Waddles, although he knew the little duck would be glad to know where he was going. But Billy Breeze didn't have time. No, sir. He had to get those rain-clouds in a hurry. It hadn't rained for so long that the roads were inches deep with dust, the Bubbling Brook was almost dry, and the Old Duck Pond was so low that the Mill Wheel couldn't turn. The Miller couldn't grind his corn, and the Miller's Boy had so much spare time to tease Granddaddy Bullfrog that the poor old gentleman frog was nearly worried to death.

"Hurry up and get those rain-clouds," shouted Granddaddy Bullfrog as Billy Breeze hurried across the Old Duck Pond.

"I wish we'd have some rain," said the "rusty, dusty" Miller, coming to the door of the Old Mill. It almost seemed as if he were speaking to Billy Breeze.

"You'll get rain pretty soon," he answered, but I guess the Miller didn't hear him, for he turned around and went inside.

By and by the rain-clouds came tumbling across the sky, as Billy Breeze pushed them headlong over one another. Mr. Merry Sun saw them coming, and hurried over to the west. But it wasn't any use. Billy Breeze drove them on so fast that in a little while Mr. Merry Sun was shut in altogether. The bright blue sky grew gray and the leaves began to whisper:

"It's going to rain! It's going to rain!"

And the grass rippled in the Sunny Meadow and murmured:

"It's going to rain! It's going to rain!"

Everybody seemed glad except, perhaps, Mr. Merry Sun. But I don't believe he minded it. He must have known that rain is just as needful as sunshine.

Pitter, patter, pitter, patter! Yes, the raindrops were falling. Chippy Chipmunk scurried into his little house and Granddaddy Bullfrog chuckled as he crawled under a sheltering leaf.

Little Jack Rabbit hopped swiftly over to the Old Bramble Patch and the Farmer's Boy turned up his collar and ran out of the Shady Forest where he had been gathering nuts.

"You're a good little boy to get home in time," said Mrs. Rabbit as her little bunny popped into the kitchen door, and the little canary bird began to sing:

"Pitter, patter, goes the rain,Making music on the pane.Draw the shades and light the lamp—Never mind the evening damp.Wind the clock, make fast the latchOf the dear Old Bramble Patch."

THE END